E ALLINGTON, RICHARD   20706 E

Hearing.

DATE DUE

MR 5 '86	MY 31 '89	SEP 2	8 1995
MR 29 '86	MAR 7 1990	NOV	5 1995
JY 19 '86	MAR 21 1991	FEB 2 3 1998	
AG 27 '86	JUL 20 1992	SEP 2 1 1999	
NO 21 '86	SEP 25 1993		
MY 18 '87	APR 06 1994		
JE 25 '87	JUL 25 1994		
JY 20 '87	AUG 9 1994		
AG 17 '87	FEB 28 1995		
NO 12 '88	MAY 3 1995		
AG 10 '88	AUG 1 1995		
MR 25 '88	AUG 22 1995		

Hearing

Library of Congress Number: 79-28387

  6 7 8 9 10 11 88 87 86 85

Printed in the United States of America.

Library of Congress Cataloging in Publication Data

Allington, Richard L
  Hearing.

  (Beginning to learn about)
  SUMMARY: Introduces about 90 sounds, such as animal, food, and people sounds and sounds that make you shiver or think of danger. Includes activities involving sound associations.
  1. Hearing — Juvenile literature. 2. Sound — Juvenile literature. [1. Sound] I. Cowles, Kathleen, joint author. II. Dober, Wayne. III. Title. IV. Series.
QP462.2.A44   152.1'5   79-28387
ISBN 0-8172-1291-4 lib. bdg.

Richard L. Allington is Associate Professor, Department of Reading, State University of New York at Albany. Kathleen Cowles is the author of several picture books.

BEGINNING TO LEARN ABOUT

HEARING

BY RICHARD L. ALLINGTON, PH.D., · AND KATHLEEN COWLES

ILLUSTRATED BY WAYNE DOBER

Raintree Childrens Books · Milwaukee · Toronto · Melbourne · London

We hear with our ears.

outer ear
(catches sounds and carries them to eardrum)

inner ear
(sends messages about sounds to the brain)

eardrum
(separates the outer and middle ear)

middle ear
(carries sounds to inner ear)

We hear sounds all the time, even in places we might think are quiet. Take one day and explore your neighborhood for its sounds. This book will show you some sounds you might hear. What other sounds can you think of? For example . . .

What sounds do you hear
that make you smile?

What loud sounds do you hear?

What soft sounds do you hear?

What sounds make you shiver?

What sounds do foods make?

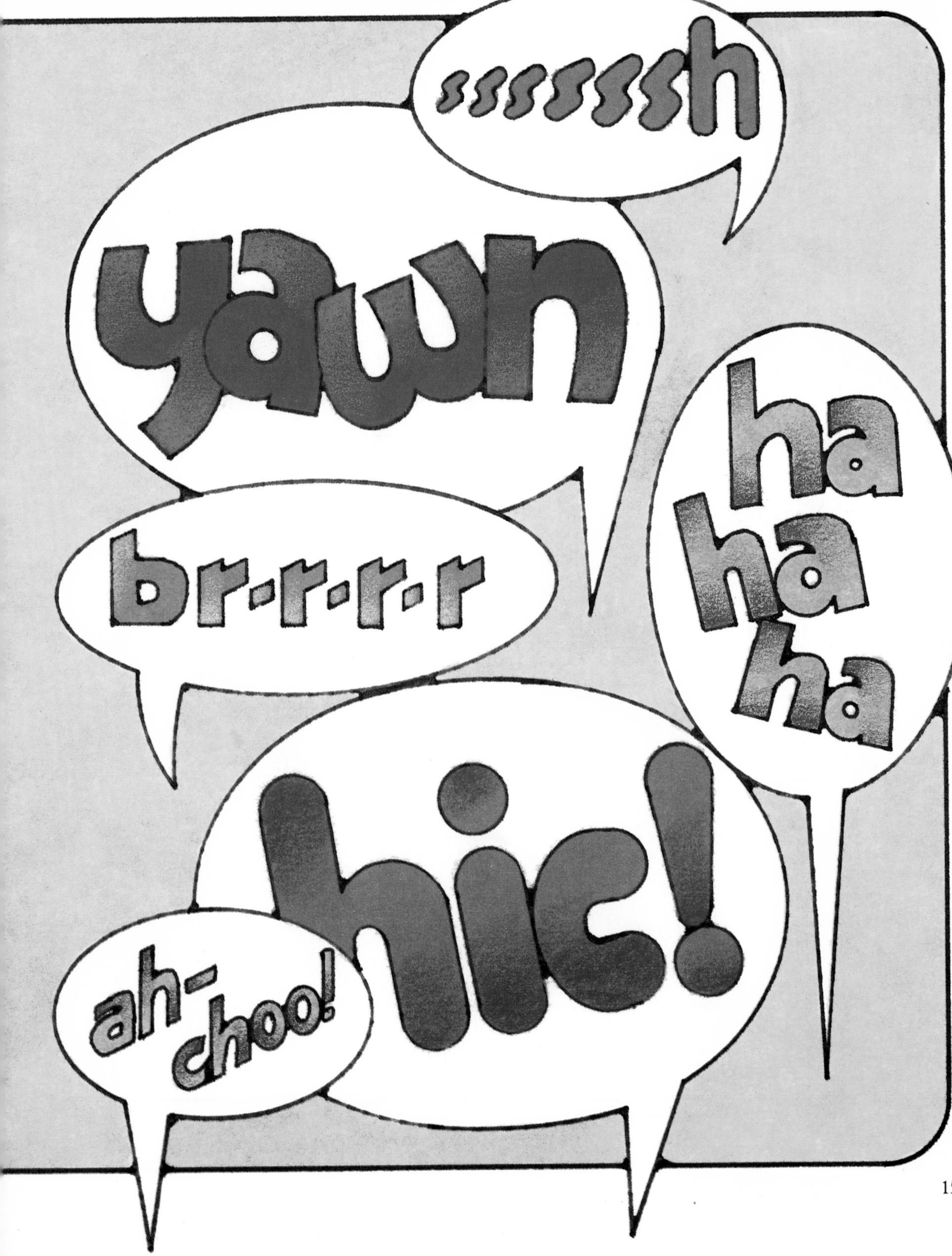
ssssssh
yawn
br-r-r-r
ha
ha
ha
ha
hic!
ah-
choo!

What sounds make you think of danger?

What animal sounds can
you hear at the zoo?

18

What animal sounds would you hear on a farm?

21

What other animal sounds can you hear?

Caroo

rat·a·
tat·tat

ribit·ribit

drip drip drip

crash

What sounds can you hear in nature?

24

What musical sounds can you hear?

27

What sounds do big machines make?

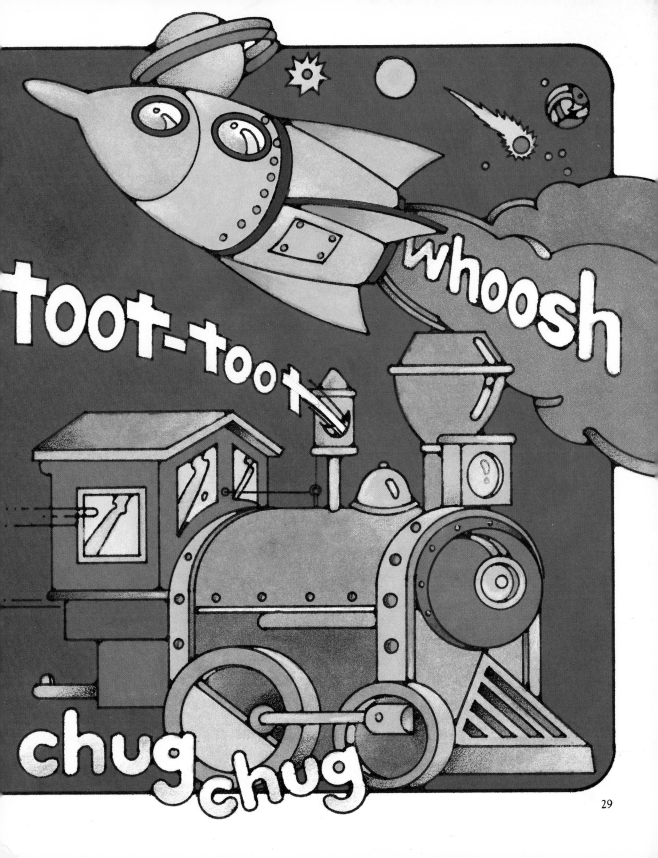

click

whir

zing

What sounds do small machines make?

31

With your finger, draw a line from each sound word to the animal that makes that sound.

Make your own book about hearing. Look through a newspaper or magazine. Find pictures of things that make sounds. Cut out the pictures. Tape or paste them onto pieces of paper. Fasten the papers together. You may ask an adult to help you.